what's the weather inside?

what's the weather inside?

poems by **karma wilson**

drawings by **barry blitt**

Margaret K. McElderry Books
New York London Toronto Sydney

Margaret K. McElderry Books

An imprint of Simon & Schuster Children's Publishing Division

1230 Avenue of the Americas, New York, New York 10020

Text copyright © 2009 by Karma Wilson

Illustrations copyright © 2009 by Barry Blitt

Book design by Debra Sfetsios

The text for this book is set in Postcard.

The illustrations for this book are rendered in pen, ink, and watercolor.

Manufactured in the United States of America

10 9 8 7 6 5 4 3 2

Library of Congress Cataloging-in-Publication Data

Wilson, Karma.

What's the weather inside? / Karma Wilson ; illustrated by Barry Blitt.

p. cm.

ISBN-13: 978-1-4169-0092-4

ISBN-10: 1-4169-0092-6

1. Children's poetry, American. 2. Humorous poetry, American. I. Blitt, Barry, ill. II. Title.

PS3623.I5854W47 2009

811'.6—dc22

2006023623

To my son, Michael—for you, I'll bake the apple pie.

To my son, David—fly on your Styrofoam wings.

To my daughter, Chrissy—your hair is as long as your list

of virtues.

You all inspire me in countless ways.

Love, Mom

For Irene and Ron

—B. B.

what's the weather inside?

What's the weather like inside?
What's the forecast say?
Is that a breeze of memory
blown in from yesterday?
Has a fog of doubt rolled in
upon the winds of change?
Or floods of creativity
with just a chance of strange?

A jolt of anger followed by
the thunder of despair?
A lilt of laughter floating
on a future bright and fair?
What's the weather like inside?
Tune in and take a look.
Is that a brainstorm coming on?
Curl up and *write* a book.

I **dare** ya

If you think poems are stupid
and poetry's a bore,
if every poem you've ever read
has almost made you snore,
and if you're sure this book's the same
as all you've read before . . .
I dare ya, yes, I dare ya: Turn the page.

MISS MUFFET'S
Revenge

Little Miss Muffet
sat on her tuffet
eating a yogurt parfait.
Along came a spider,
who sat down beside her.
She squished it
and flicked it away.

what your Dog
Might Be Thinking

I love to pee on the flower bed.
I love to eat things smelly and dead.
I love the smell of putridness.
I love to frolic in rottenness.
I love to bury my bones in a hole.
I love to drink from the toilet bowl.
I love to munch what the garbage man misses.
I love to give my people kisses. *SLURP!*

what your cat
Might Be Thinking

I'm the center of the universe.
I'm all-out royalty.
There really isn't anyone
who's near as good as me.
And everything that's ever done
is done just for my bidding.
And I shall banish anyone
I do not deem befitting.
Laps were made to be my throne,
and hands were made to pet me.
And anything I want to do,
of course, you have to let me.
And if you open up a book,
then that's to lay my head on.
And if you put your sweater down,
well, that's for me to shed on.
And if you plant a pretty plant,
well, that's for me to chew.
And if you bring a puppy home,
well, that's the end of you.

what your Hamster
Might Be Thinking

RUN
RUN
RUN
RUN!
Through the kitchen
down the hall
RUN
RUN
RUN
RUN!
Must . . . escape . . . the . . .
plastic . . . ball . . .

Naps

I don't like naps.
In fact, I hate 'em . . .
unless my baby brother
takes 'em.

Changing Time

It's changing time for brother.
Pew.
It's time to change that diaper.
Ew.
Dirty, stinky, icky poo.
It's changing time again.

Somebody change him now!
Who?
Will someone change my brother?
You?
Me? Gee, it's not so bad.
It's not quite changing time.
Whew!

Alligator Purse

"Oh, dahling, don't you love my purse?
It's genuine alligator."
She said that just this morning,
but then a little later
she reached inside for something
and it ate her.

Inside a Tornado

I wonder what it might be like
inside a big tornado.
Floating free, like Dorothy,
you'd ride the rushing flow.
Twirling, swirling, whirling,
maybe shouting as you go . . .

"HELP! I DO NOT WANT TO BE

INSIDE THIS BIG TORNADO!"

Mother's Day

I went all out for Mother's Day
and picked my mom a sweet bouquet:
yellow, purple, pink, and red,
right from our neighbor's flower bed!

I gave them to my mom and smiled.
(She's so lucky I'm her child.)
She saw them and began to sneeze.
Oops! My mom has allergies.

Regretful Sue

Regretful Sue, it's sad but true,
regretted everything she did.
She regretted every word she said
and every thought that crossed her head.
She regretted every friend she made
and every game she ever played.
She regretted every place she went
and every single cent she spent.
Each job she got would bring regret;
she regretted the ones she didn't get.
She regretted up to the day she died
and on that day she cried and cried.
That's when Sue, I'm sorry to say,
regretted regretting her life away.

ONOMATOPOEIA
(On-oh-ma-toe-PEE-ah)

Oh, that ONOMATOPOEIA—
what a fabulous idea.
　　It makes my heart
　　　go *Rappity-tap!*
Makes my fingers
go *Snappity-snap!*
　　Makes my toes
　　go *Tippety-tap!*
Makes my hands
go *Clappity-clap!*
　　Oh, that onomatopoeia—
　　what a fabulous idea*!*
Sounds so lovely
when you tell it,
but goodness,
try to spell it!

TIC
TIC

SCRITCH

BZZZ

VROOM

WELCOME TO ONOMATOPOEIA

E, I, E, I, Oh No!

The spelling rule says . . .
i before *e*, except after *c*,
or when sounding like "ay"
as in "neighbor" or "weigh."
Sounds like a breeze
until you spell "seize."
Then it's *e* before *i*,
and I'd like to know why.
I think it's *weird*, cruel, and unfair.
It makes me feel *feisty* and mad.
I have *neither* the time nor the *leisure*
to learn all the words that go bad.
Either this rule is completely unfit,
or certain words are **counterfeit**.

A List of **Lovely** words

Sunshine,
twilight,
heavenly,
moonlight,
butterfly,
chamomile,
rainbow,
daffodil,
hummingbird,
turtledove,
faith,
hope,
love.

A List of **ugly** words

Maggot,
neglected,
rotten,
rejected,
traitor,
homicide,
moron,
petrified,
hellish,
desecrate,
death,
war,
hate.

The Bad Hair Day

The other day when I got up,
my hair was in distress.
One glance into the bathroom mirror
revealed a frightful mess!

I tried to comb my frazzled hair,
but it refused to stay.
My mother looked me up and down
and said, "A bad hair day."

So I decided then and there
to end my hairy gloom.
I got my mother's scissors
and I tiptoed to my room.

I clipped and snipped my wayward hair,
until my mother called.
She took one look and passed out cold,
to see her daughter bald.

Magic Carpet

I have a magic carpet.
He's such a lovely sight.
We'd fly, we would,
if we only could . . .
> A magic carpet really should.
> But he's afraid of heights.

If
I Could
Pick My Nose

If I were free to pick my nose—
I've given it some thought—
I wouldn't pick a different one.
I like the one I've got.

The Beast and the Beauty

Once there was an ugly beast
with an ugly body and ugly face
and he lived in an ugly house of sticks
shrouded in shame and disgrace.

And once there was a beautiful lady
with beautiful dresses and beautiful hair.
She lived in a beautiful mansion of stone
without any worries or care.

The beautiful lady put on her cloak
and went for a stroll one day.
She came to the ugly beast on the path,
and she turned her eyes away.

"Might we be friends?" he ventured to ask.
And she laughed and she laughed till she cried.
The beast, it seems, had a beautiful heart,
but the lady was ugly inside.

Betty

I do not have a Teddy Bear.
Instead I have a Betty Bear.
It seemed a better name to me
because my bear is she, not he.

Critics

I wrote a story, a wonderful story—
the bestest story I ever saw.
I showed my mom and she liked it too,
but she thought it had one flaw.

She liked the beginning, she liked it fine,
but the ending she thought could be better.
So I changed my story like she said—
down to the very last letter.

I showed my dad, he liked it too.
He said, "It's a fabulous tale.
But it has one tiny problem, son.
I think the beginning is stale."

So I changed my story like he said—
I got every word just so.
Then I showed my uncle the story too,
and my uncle said, "You know?

I like the story very much.
It's funny and full of suspense.
But it seems to me that middle part
just doesn't make much sense."

So I changed my story like *everyone* said—
and now it's a terrible bore.
Since writing for others instead of myself,
writing's no fun anymore.

Golden Eggs

The goose that laid
the golden eggs
was sad as any goose could be.
She'd rather have
one fluffy chick
than a *million* golden eggs, you see.

Pot of Rainbow

A pot of gold would be okay.
I'd like it better, though,
if instead of the pot of gold
you got to keep the rainbow.

word Play

Words at play, words at play,
oh, what a magical, mystical day.
They romp and rhyme and alliterate,
they tantalize and titillate.
They heave a heap of hyperbole
in a tale as tall as a redwood tree.
They help you speak when you've nothing to say,
when the words get together to play.

Words at play, words at play,
wonderfully witty in all their ways.
For a myth they make an analogy
as fresh as a peach in an apple tree.
They add an acronym or two,
some TLC and IOU.
Oh, they're getting carried away,
those mischievous marvelous words at play.

Words at play, words at play,
they've chased the ho-hum blues away.
They're giving us prose and poems and puns.
They tap the teacher and just for fun
they say, "Madam, have a palindrome!"
then scamper off to their just-write home
in the pages of books, and there they'll stay
and all get together to play, play, play.

The Problem with Pepper Spray

I saw a bear!
I climbed a tree.
That bear, he climbed
up after me.
I clutched a can
of pepper spray.
That bear just roared
and said, "Hurray!"
I told that bear,
"You'd better halt!"
That bear pulled out
a jar of salt!
He grabbed my spray
and said, "Oh, joy.
I just love salt-
and-peppered boy!"

Oh, Brother

If r were taken out of *brother*,
your brother would just be a bother.
You say your brother *is* a bother?
There he goes to tell your father.

Oh, brother.

Please Peel My Peach

Fuzzy fruit I think is best
when fruit is more
and fuzz is less.

Sass

Don't sass your mom.
Don't sass your dad.
Don't sass your teacher,
'cause sassin's bad.

Don't sass Aunt Alma
or Uncle Richard
or Pastor Steve
or Old Man Pritchard.

And someday when
you're thirty-two,
they'll tell the kids
to not sass you.

what the New Gnu Knew . . .

A gnu was born, a brand-new gnu.
And this is what that new gnu knew.
She knew she loved her mama gnu.
She knew her mama loved her, too.
The new gnu grew and grew and grew.
But what she knew when she was new
would help to get the young gnu through
until she had her own new gnu,
who knew she loved her mama gnu
and knew her mama loved her, too.

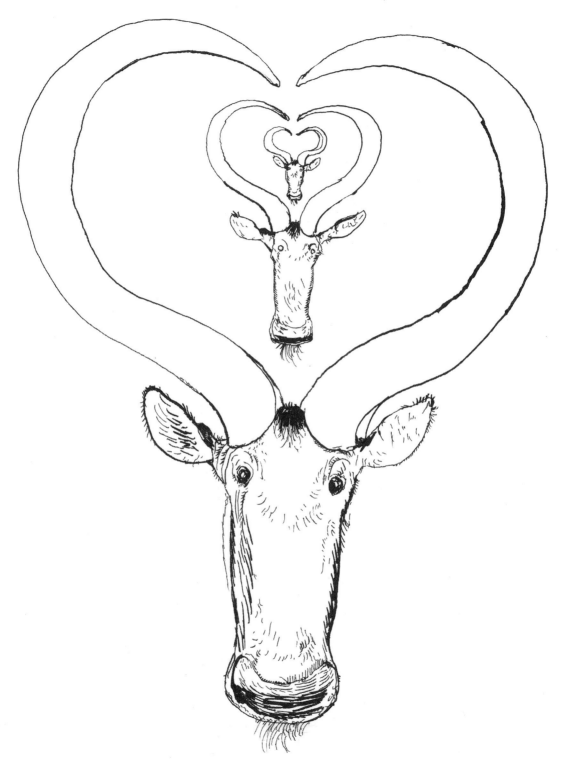

Forgotten Poems

Last night as I lay in my bed
a pretty poem popped in my head.
I should have written it down, I guess,
but I was sleepy, I confess.
And now the poem has disappeared
from that space between my ears.
It flew away, or so it seems,
to the land of forgotten poems and dreams.
This has happened, I just know it,
to lots of other drowsy poets.
All those poems, the good and bad,
words now lost we might have had.
I wish I had a magic net
to catch the poems that people forget.

UNwrapped

The mummy said of his mummy wraps,
"They squeeze, they press, they bind.
In these things I can't relax.
I think I need to unwind."

But once he was there out in the air,
he was chilled right down to the bone.
So he wound himself back up again.
I think that wraps up this poem.

Dental Anxiety

I have to go to the dentist's office.
I really don't want to go.
I'm scared as can be. It's torture to me.
That place is a danger, you know.

I have to go to the dentist's office.
Why can't I just stay in bed?
I'd rather be here than anywhere near
that building that fills me with dread.

I have to go to the dentist's office.
I *am* the dentist, it's true.
But that place is a fright, my patients all bite,
and I might lose a finger or two!

Perfectly Prissy Priscilla

She's perfectly prissy Priscilla.
  She's prissy as prissy can be.
  She smells like perfumed vanilla
  and she only wears pink fluffery.

She will not touch anything yucky.
  She never makes mud cakes or pies.
  She never gets muddy or mucky.
  And if she spills something she cries.

Priscilla will only play dress-up.
  She likes to pretend she's a queen.
  She makes all of us clean her mess up.
  (She's much, much too prissy to clean!)

"When I am grown up," says Priscilla,
  "I'll wear only diamonds and fur."
  She's perfectly prissy Priscilla.
  I'm perfectly glad I'm not her!

Too **Tall** Tim

Too Tall Tim is tall as can be,
at least as tall as a hickory tree.
And when he rides his little horse,
he's much too tall to sit, of course.
So instead he stands astride,
and as the two go take a ride,
all the townsfolk watch the show,
Tim walking tall with his horse below.

Santa ISN'T Real

Santa isn't real. *No, Santa isn't real.*
No fat man brings a zillion toys
to all the nicest girls and boys.
Santa isn't real.

I know he isn't real. I'm sure he isn't real.
No reindeers fly, they don't have wings.
And elves aren't making toys and things.
Santa isn't real.

I'm sure he isn't real. Quite sure he isn't real.
He can't fit down your fireplace,
a chimney doesn't have the space.
No, Santa isn't real.

Santa isn't real. He really isn't real.
I'm sure of this. In fact, I know
'cause Easter Bunny told me so.
And Easter Bunny's real!

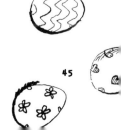

45

Dental **Hygiene**

My dentist said to floss each night.
I'm pretty sure I do it right.
I floss each tooth in my dog's head.
I do it like the dentist said.
I brush his teeth and floss him too.

I want to keep his teeth like new.
Then I use that floss on me.
The toothbrush, too, because, you see,
I brush and floss with utmost care,
but me and my dog always share.

Styrofoam wings

Mom got a package, a great big package.
Inside were these Styrofoam things.
And I thought to myself, "I just might fly
if I made some Styrofoam wings."

So I got myself some wrapping tape
and a ball of old kite string.
And I put those things upon my back,
and I made myself some wings.

My parents said, "How very cute,
but, honey, they won't fly."
I said, "They might, they surely might.
To know I'll have to try."

My brother said, "You nutty kid.
You know those things won't fly."
I said, "I don't know that at all,
and I won't until I try."

And my little sister looked at me
with great big trusting eyes.
And she said, "Please bring me something back
from wherever you go fly."

And then she said, "Good-bye."

I went outside and I flapped real fast,
I watched as the larks went flying past,
I jumped to give myself a blast,
and then I started to fly at last.

I flew through the sky above the trees,
I fluttered along with the birds and the bees,
I felt the cool of the gentle breeze,
and I knew I could fly wherever I pleased.

And all because I tried.

I looked upon the moon's
face as he arose,
and wondered does he ever
get boogers in his nose?
I have never seen one,
but he's rather far away.
Perhaps he simply blows his nose
upon the Milky Way!

A NoSy QueStioN for the MOON

Petting
Zoo

One turtle,
two frogs,
three tiny pollywogs.
Four mice,
five rats,
six baby muskrats.
Seven snakes,
eight ants
in the pockets
of my pants!

My
Yummy
Valentine!

I like getting valentines.
In fact, I think they're dandy.
I like getting valentines.
But just the kind with candy.

DEcaffeinated

My mom is out of coffee.
The day is looking black.
You've never seen quite anything
like Mom's caffeine attack.
She gets a splitting headache
and starts to yell a lot.
There's nothing quite as scary
as an empty coffeepot.
My mom is out of coffee,
the day is starting bad.
But it will go from bad to worse
as soon as we tell Dad.

Fishin' Wishin'

Oh, I'm wishin' I were fishin'
and my toes they were a-swishin'
in that pond with all the fish in,
that old pond where I go fishin'.

And I'm wishin' I were dishin'
up the fish that I had caught.
Oh, I'm wishin' I were fishin'—
but I'm not!

Dodgeball

Don't play dodgeball on a cliff.
Do you wonder why?
Because it's not a good idea
unless you learn to fly.

P.E.?

We run in P.E.
We run and we sweat.
We jump in P.E.,
and sweat some more yet.
We play in P.E.
and perspire a lot.
When working that hard,
the gym feels so hot.
And all of that sweating
is stinky, it's true.
They call it P.E. It should be P.U.

The Jesse James Song

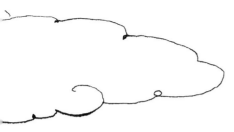

Jesse James, Jesse James,
let's all write a song about Jesse James.
Now, there was a man of renown and acclaim,
that old-time hero, Jesse James.

Jesse James, Jesse James,
he had glory and he had fame.
What did he do, that Jesse James,
that set the whole wide world aflame?

Jesse James, Jesse James—
what great things did Jesse do?
Cheated, robbed, and killed folks too?
He did that stuff? Is all that true?

Jesse James, Jesse James,
let's not write a song about Jesse James.
Let's sing out loud and sing out strong
for someone who actually deserves a song.

The wind

The wind has blown my laugh away.
Where it blew I cannot say.

I hope it flew to someone blue
                    and cheered them up for a minute or two.

DishwaSher

Our dishwasher broke.
Mom chose another.
Sadly, it's me,
and not my big brother.

washing machine

My mom is cruel, my mom is mean.
She put stuffed bunny in the washing machine.
And there he sloshed round and round
                and round and round until . . .
                                he drowned.

Sit-Downs

I want to play in the park.
    My parents want to sit down.
I want to splash in the pool.
    My parents want to sit down.
I want to hide and be found.
    My parents want to sit down.
I want to run through the grass.
    My parents want to sit down.
And everything I want to do,
    they still just want to sit down.
Why are they called grown-ups?
    They should be called sit-downs.

what I missed

She's my sister and I missed her
when she went away to camp.
She's my sister, so I missed her
quite a lot.
She's my sister and I missed her,
but now that she's come back,
why I missed my sister,

       I forget!

Bad medicine

My sister caught a pill bug.
She thought it was a pill.
My sister ate the pill bug.
And now my sister's ill.

Tortoise Race

This race is slow
as races go.
It is a tortoise
race, you know.
Creeping . . . stalling . . .
barely crawling,
on and on they go.

But in this race
it's no disgrace
to have a hardly
moving pace.
Stopping . . . slowing . . .
barely going.
Last one wins
first place!

Treasure chest

Ned found a chest in the attic.
And now he is simply ecstatic.
He says it holds a great treasure
with value too awesome to measure!

Musty clothes, dusty shoes,
worn-out rusty swords.
A broken watch, an old shoehorn,
and three half-rotten boards.
Faded pictures, holey hats,
a nest of teensy baby rats.

"All this stuff is great!" said Ned.
"It's just old trash," our grandma said.
Grandpa winked. "Well, one thing's true,
treasure depends on your point of view."

Say **Cheese**

My mom is taking pictures,
and she asked for me to smile.
But I just don't feel happy,
and it's really quite a trial
to smile when you're cranky
and you're wanting just to frown.
She said, "Oh, please, I ask you—
turn that frowning upside down."
But I don't wanna smile.
I'm not gonna, you can bet.
Who would want to smile
when they're grumpy and upset?
Mom wants me to smile.
But I'm grouchy and annoyed.
Mom said, "I could ground you."
So now I'm overjoyed.

Give
Me a
Break!

I broke my arm and got a cast.
And when I went to school,
all my friends were quite impressed.
They thought my cast was cool.

The whole class signed it, everyone,
and most of them were nice.
Jenny wrote, "Get better soon,"
and "Awesome dude!" wrote Brice.

Andrea wrote, "U-R-Neat!"
and Josh wrote, "Way to go!"
Everyone wrote something good,
except for Betty Jo.

In bright red ink she wrote real big,
"TO JONATHAN THE PEST."
But I changed the *P* into a *B*.
I guess that makes me BEST.

Herbivores

Herb went in the woods one day.
And now Herb is no more.
He came to an end, or so some say,
when he met an herbivore.

Carnivores

Do carnivores like carnivals?
They do, but not for the rides.
Carnivores like carnivals
for the tasty children inside.

Omnivores

Omnivores are ominous.
They fill every heart with dismay.
For if you are meat, or if you are plant,
you'd make them a yummy buffet.

A Perfect world

I'm glad it's not a perfect world
with perfect boys
and perfect girls.
With perfect poems
and perfect songs
and perfect paths
to walk along.
With perfect flowers
in perfect beds
and perfect hills
with perfect sleds.
For in that world,
there'd never be
room for poor imperfect me.

The Simple Things

If you've ever hiked for miles on end
on a trail that twists and climbs and bends,
and you finally stop to take a rest—
well, that's when simple things are best.
Jerky tastes like filet mignon.
An apple tastes like apple pie.
That hard old rock that you're sitting on
feels like the fluffiest cloud in the sky.
A hawk on the wing is a glorious thing.
Water is sweet like fruit off the vine.
And earth is almost like heaven above;
you feel so wonderfully, perfectly fine.

Don't Eat yellow Snow!

A while back my father warned me,
"DON'T EAT YELLOW SNOW!"
I asked him why and he replied,
"Because I told you so!"
He said, "It's sure to make you sick.
Don't even try one bite."
He sounded pretty serious,
and so I said, "All right."
Then one day my little sister
almost did the worst.
She would have eaten yellow snow
had I not stopped her first!
But right before she took a taste,
I saved her just in time.

I threw her lemon snow cone down
and bought her kiwi-lime.

Granny's Flapjacks

Granny's in the kitchen making towering stacks
of the finest, most divine-est, fat-n-fluffy flapjacks.
When Granddad Jack grabs a cake off the stack,
it crashes on his plate with a thundering *CRACK!*

Granny's in the kitchen, but something's the matter
with the fixins Granny put in that flapjack batter.
Cement for flour? Glue for molasses?
When Granny starts cookin', she should put on her glasses.

Chrissy's Hair

Chrissy's hair, it grew so long.
It grew one hundred feet.
It dragged behind her when she walked,
and covered up the street.
And as it dragged along behind,
it picked up many things—
animals of every kind,
both furry and with wings.
A snowshoe hare got stuck in there
with a rare white arctic fox.
And toys and trinkets tangled up
in Chrissy's golden locks.
Bikes and trikes and garbage, too,
got matted in the mess.
I lost my favorite piggy bank—
in Chrissy's hair, I guess.
A hitchhiker once hitched a ride
on the tail of Chrissy's hair.
We don't know just how far he got.
He might still be in there!
But Chrissy will not cut her hair
an inch, for heaven's sake.
But she moans and groans most every day
that her head has a terrible ache!

Picky Kids

Betty will not eat spaghetti,
Lou will not eat stew.
Cousin Drake will not eat steak.
(He says it's hard to chew.)
Hanna will not eat banana,
not a single bit.
If she gets some on her plate,
she throws a holy fit!
But I'm not picky like these kids.
Not me! My name is Mandy,
and I don't have a single problem
eating lots of candy.

Camplaining

I don't like to camp
out in the sticks.
Too many fleas
too many ticks
too many bugs
too many bees
too many noises
that creak in the trees.
Too many rocks
too many snakes
too many leeches
that lurk in the lakes.
Too many skunks
too many bears
too many crawlies
that creep in my hairs.
Too much sunshine
too much raining
and Dad always says,
"Too much complaining."

Give the **Cat a Bath**

I tried to give my cat a bath.
I ran the water in the tub.
I grabbed a sponge to help me scrub.
I got my cat, to put her in.
But then . . .

SCRATCH

GROWL

HISSSSS

HOWL

DON'T TRY GIVING YOUR CAT A BATH.

MOM'S Diet

My mom is on a diet.
I'm telling you, it's rough.
She's always cooking greens and beans
and other "healthy" stuff.
Whenever we go out to eat,
she gets the diet size.
But at this rate she won't lose weight.

My mom steals half my fries!

Gophers wearing Loafers

Gophers wearing loafers—
that would be a silly sight.
Or a reindeer wearing rain gear
on a dark and stormy night.
Tomcats wearing top hats
to a fancy ballroom dance.
Or a cuckoo in a tutu
sporting flowered underpants.
A turkey gone berserky
while she wears a frilly dress.
Oh, if animals wore clothing,
my, this world would be a mess.
But it could be a whole lot worse,
why, some would say a sin,
if people *didn't* wear their clothes
and ran around in skin!

Rattle tales

Never shake a rattlesnake
to see if it will rattle.
And if you see your brother try it,
go ahead and tattle!

The Pits

My sister claimed a giant monster
lurked beneath her bed.
I laughed and sneered, "I don't believe
a single word you've said."
She shrugged. "Okay. I dare you then,
trade rooms with me tonight."

Now here I sit in a monster pit.
I hate when my sister is right.

Pilot

My brother said, "I want to fly.
I want to travel way up high.
I want to skim the deep blue sky
and zooooom up to the Milky Way!"

I said, "You'll never do it, Mike.
You're only just a little tyke.
Why, you can't even ride your bike!"
He flapped his arms and flew away.

The MANNERS Poem

She doesn't say "thank you."
She doesn't say "please."
She never says "Bless you"
when somebody sneezes.

She leaves her mouth open
when chewing her food.
There's no doubt about it—
our granny is rude.

My Dad's
Tattoo

My dad's tattoo
is faded blue.
A gorgeous girl
named Betty Lu.
It says, "I'll always
cherish you."
But I'm quite sure
that isn't true.
Dad loves Mom,
whose name is Sue.
(She doesn't love
my dad's tattoo.)

N'mores

Camping out last night, I said,
"S'mores! S'mores! S'mores!"
I savored every bite and cried,
"S'more, s'more, s'more!"
That sweet marshmallow goo. I called,
"S'more, s'more! S'more!"
I'd only eaten two and yelled,
"S'more, s'more, s'more!"
That chocolate was divine. I screamed,
"S'more, s'more, s'more!"
I'd only eaten nine and shrieked,
"S'more, s'more, s'more!"
I ate another ten. That's when . . .
I started feeling poor.
My face turned kind of green and then
my stomach got *real* sore.
My insides started rumbling.
I puked and puked s'more.
All night I lay there grumbling,
"*N'more, n'more, n'more!*"

It's awful
and deplorable.
It's terrible
and horrible.
Mom called me
adorable
in front of
all my friends.

The **Alphabet** Game

On the road we play
the alphabet game.
I think that game
is totally lame.
I can't find letters
of the alphabet—
I haven't learned
to read them yet!
The alphabet game's
no fun for me.
It's not my fault
I'm only three.

Magic Homework wand!

I'll never get my homework done.
I've tried for hours and hours.
I wish I had a homework wand
with magic homework powers.
I'd zap my paper and *BOOM! KAZAM!*
my homework would be done.
Then I'd go outside and play
and have a load of fun.
Mom said, "There *is* a homework wand.
You wield one every day.
It's called a *pencil*, silly one.
Use it. Then go play."

Nothing Fair About It

A robot's hitting Amber Lynn.
I think she has a broken shin.

Miss Meeker slipped in yellow slime.
Roberto grew a five-pound lime.

Matt is mad. He's lost his bugs.
Rachel sat on banana slugs.

A great volcano blew its lid
and killed poor Edward's mutant squid.

There's frog guts stuck in Jenny's hair.

Just one more year at the science fair.

How Much Sea?

How much sea could a sea snake see
if a sea snake could see sea?
Seems to me it is simple, you see,
since a sea snake can see sea.
So much sea, he may simply be
sick, sick, sick of seeing sea, sea, sea!

Mary Had an Appetite

Mary had a little lamb.
She fed him every day.
She fed him grains
and yummy oats
and sweet alfalfa hay.
Little did her sheep suspect
he'd never be a ram.
Mary's very favorite food
was juicy rack of lamb.

Red-Letter Day

Hurray! Hurray! It's a red-letter day!
My teacher gave me a big, fat A
in bright-red ink and uppercase—
and beside it, a great, big smiley face!
She asked us to write what we wanted to be.
That was an easy paper for me.
I said the highest goal I could reach,
of course, would be to teach.

Rapunzel, Rapunzel

Rapunzel, Rapunzel,
don't be a dope.
Cut off your hair
and make your own rope.

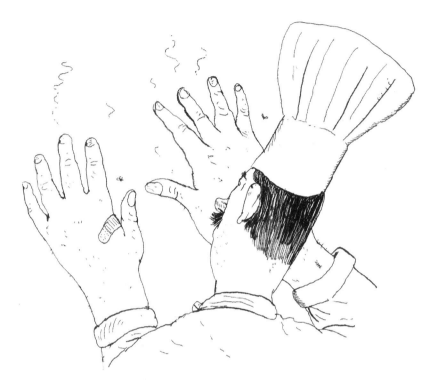

Patty-cake

Patty-cake, patty-cake, baker's man,
bake me a cake as fast as you can.
But please before you pat it,
go and wash your hands!

Substitute
Teacher

Our substitute teacher
is mean as can be.
He never gives grades
that are higher than C.
He won't let us talk,
he yells and he screeches.
He bangs on his desk
and stomps as he teaches.
He's not very nice.
We call him "the brute."
Let's get a sub
for the substitute!

Take
That
Back!

My brother is rotten.
My brother is mean.
My brother is spoiled
and rude and obscene.
My brother is pesky.
My brother is nuts.
My brother is loony
and I hate his guts.
What's that you say?
I'm right? You agree?
Tell me you're sorry!
I'm counting to three.
Nobody picks on my
brother but me!

Leftovers

Leftovers again.
They taste so bad.
Food that is left
is oh-so-sad.
Icky leftovers.
Oh, I'm mad.
I guess I'll eat them,
but just a tad.
I hate leftovers,
and so does Dad.
Oh, leftover pizza?
That's not so bad.

Some Birthday

No one remembered my birthday today.
There's no yummy ice cream with cake.
No candles to blow on, no spankings to grow on,
no pretty piñatas to break.

No one remembered my birthday today.
There aren't any gifts to be found.
No presents wrapped neatly, no ribbons tied sweetly,
and no friends or family around.

No one remembered my birthday today.
There's no party hat just my size.
I'm sad and alone, I guess I'll go home,
since nobody loves me . . .

A Dog for Melissa

Melissa wants a puppy dog,
but she says he must be quiet.
He shouldn't bark or chew things up
or cause a general riot.

He shouldn't scratch his private parts
or dig holes anywhere.
He shouldn't shed on Melissa's bed.
(She's allergic to doggy hair.)

And Melissa doesn't want to walk
her doggy every day.
And wherever Melissa puts her pup,
that's where he'd better stay.

Melissa wants a puppy dog.
I've found one she'll adore.
The sweetest little stuffed toy dog
from the stuffed toy animal store.

Greener Grass

One horse said to the other,
"Your grass is a lot more green."
"Naaay, friend," said the first horse.
"You've the greenest grass I've seen."
The second horse said, "No waaaay.
This grass is brown and wilted."
The first horse got a bright idea
and said with his big head tilted,
"Saaay, let's trade. I'll hop the fence
if you like my grass so well.
You eat here and I'll eat there."
And the second horse said, "Swell."
So they jumped their fences and started to munch,
but after a minute had passed,
the first horse neighed, "I am afraid
you have the greener grass."

Not-So-Hot
Dogs

If you eat your hot dogs cold,
I guess they're not so hot.
We shouldn't call them hot dogs
when hot is what they're not.
So if you eat your hot dogs cold—
plain or tucked in bread—
you shouldn't call them hot dogs.
Call them chilly dogs instead.

Gus

On our bus
a guy named Gus
was big and mean
and picked on us.
He yelled a lot.
He liked to cuss.
He said my brother
smelled like pus!
My mom found out
and made a fuss.
She got that guy
kicked off our bus.
They fired old
bus driver Gus.

If You Were a Giant

Imagine if you were a thousand feet tall!
You might cause an earthquake if you were to fall.
Just one of your sneezes could generate breezes
that blew away cities, the buildings and all.

Imagine if you weighed three tons, give or take.
For taking a bath, you'd need a large lake.
And your birthday would be a real tragedy
'cause no one could bake such an oversized cake.

If you were a giant, as big as could be,
why, you could look down on the redwood trees!
And I'd be your friend, by your side to the end
(in hopes that you wouldn't get angry with me).

Tae Kwon **DON'T**

I learned to kick
in tae kwon do.
I learned some punches
I can throw.
I learned to stretch.
I learned to shout.
I learned what
tae kwon do's about.
My teacher taught me.
What a guy.
He said to kick him
in the thigh.
I learned my aim's
a foot too high.

OOPS

ow

Sunday's
Sundaes

If I were queen, I would decree
that every Sunday we should be
allowed to eat throughout the day
only ice cream sundaes.

If I were queen, I might suggest
that sunny days are always best
to eat cold food throughout the day,
like yummy ice cream sundaes.

And if, like me, you love ice cream,
don't you wish that I *were* queen?

Craving Coffee

Mom won't let me try a cup
of hot and steamy coffee.
She says I can't, till I grow up,
drink dark and dreamy coffee.
It's been one of my oldest wishes
to drink coffee . . . so delicious.
Who cares if it's not nutritious?
I want *one* sip of coffee!
And so, while Mom is on the phone,
I sneak her cup of coffee.
I tiptoe off and sit alone
and try one taste of coffee.
And then I choke and hack and cough,
it makes my taste buds all fall off!
That stuff belongs in an old pig trough.
Gross, disgusting coffee.

Haunted House

We go peeking, peeking, peeking
in the broken-down, old window.

We go sneaking, sneaking, sneaking
up the stairway, through the door.

Old boards start cracking, creaking
as we walk on tippy-toe.

A mouse starts squealing, squeaking
in his hole there by the floor.

Wait, a voice is speaking!
Deep and dark, it says so clear,

"WHY ARE YOU HERE?
WHY ARE YOU HERE!?
WHY ARE YOU HERE!?!?"

We go shrieking, shrieking, shrieking
down the stairs, back out the door!

And I promise, we aren't going to
that haunted house no more!

Breakfast in Bed

I made my mommy breakfast.
A gift for Mother's Day!
I served it to her piping hot
upon a pretty tray.
I picked her dandelions,
the prettiest bouquet.
Just a little touch of mine
to brighten up her day!
Then I watched while Mommy tried
my favorite recipe:
tuna cakes with berry jam.
That's my specialty!
She took a bite and then declared,
"Mmmm . . . they taste just right."
I must have made them perfect.
She was full with just one bite!

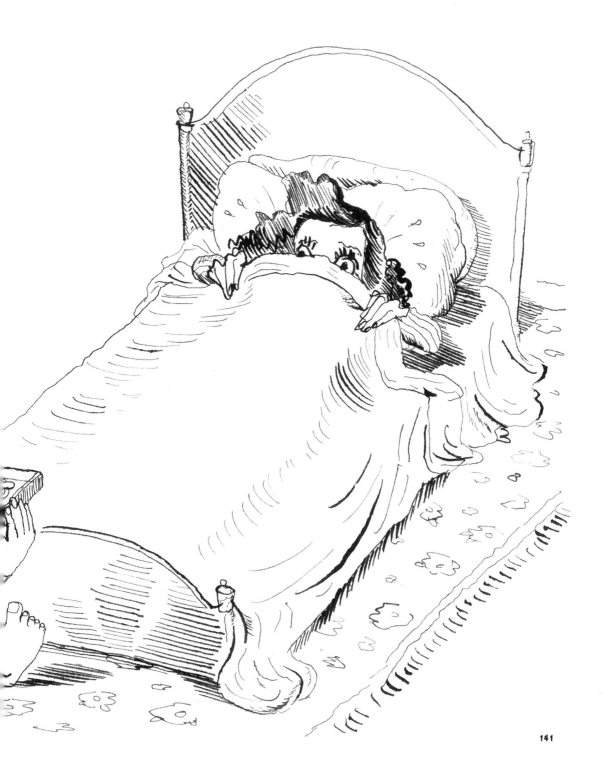

"Did not!"
"Did so!"
"Uh-huh!"
"Heck, no!"
"I'm right!"
"No way!"
"Who says?"
"I say!"
"Break it up,
this isn't right!"
I hate it when
my parents fight.

The Argument

Silly willy

Silly Willy was a clown.
Silly Willy liked to frown.
Silly Willy wasn't very silly.
Really.

Friends for Dinner

If you plan to have friends for dinner,
I think you should take my advice.
It's okay to munch, but I have a hunch
that eating your friends isn't nice.

Fly ball, high ball,
sailin'-through-the-sky ball.
Why-oh-why-did-you-
have-to-hit-my-eye ball!

DON'T **TICKLE** ME!

Don't tickle me, please.
Don't tickle my toes.
Don't tickle my elbows.
Don't tickle my nose.
Don't tickle my ribs.
Don't tickle my knees.
Don't tickle my armpit.
Don't tickle me, please.
It just makes me cackle
and chuckle and giggle.
I laugh till I cry,
I squirm and I wiggle.
I roll on the ground
and I snicker a ton.
Don't tickle me, please.
It's not *any* fun.

I'm STARVING, Ma!

I'm STARVING, Ma, I need to eat
something tasty, something sweet,
a warm and fresh-baked gooey treat.
I'm STARVING, Ma, I need to eat.

I'm STARVING, Ma, I just might die
if you don't bake an apple pie.
I'm getting thin, I'll say good-bye.
I'm STARVING, Ma, I just might die.

I'm STARVING, Ma, and I confess
if I don't eat I'll STARVE to death.
A healthy snack? No more, no less?
I'm not that hungry now, I guess.

what I Learned in Science . . .

Teacher taught us something new
today in science class.
Everything on earth is either
liquid, solid, or gas.
She said to write a paper
with examples of all three.
While at the dinner table
the answer came to me!
A liquid is the milk I drink.
One down, two to go.
A solid is the chili beans.
And gas? Well, that I know.
When Dad is eating chili beans,
it always comes to pass—
in just an hour, maybe two,
you wait, and he'll have gas!

TOM

Tom is my canary.
He's a very lovely bird.
He sings the most delightful ditties
you have ever heard.
No matter how upset you are,
his tune will make you calm.
He trills and tweets, "Peep, peep, peep!"
We call him Peeping Tom.

At the Movies

He keeps crunching, munching, chewing—
and I cannot hear the movie.
I can only sit here stewing.
But I cannot hear the movie.
His popcorn makes such a racket
that I cannot hear the movie.
Could he hurry up and snack it
so that I can hear the movie?
Oh, FORGET IT! I am moving!
"Sorry, oops, excuse me."
Ah, that's so much better!
I can finally hear the movie.
But that lady's hat is giant—
so I cannot see the movie.

Family Reunion

Aunt Betty wants a kiss.
Aunt Charlotte wants a hug.
Cousin Harold stands there
in the doorway looking smug.
Mother says I'm slouching
and could I stand up straighter?
Oh, look, it's Cousin Sue,
and I'm pretty sure I hate her.
There is Uncle Donald.
He teases, "You grew smaller!"
My baby cousin Matthew
sees my dad and starts to holler.
Mom is taking pictures,
but no one wants to smile.
I ask my grandpa, "Why
are these reunions such a trial?"
Grandpa winks and says, "Just wait a while."

After a while . . .

We all ate lots of burgers,
and we drank the fruit punch gone.
The family spends the afternoon
out lounging on the lawn.
Me and Sue and Harold
are playing tag together.
The grown-ups sit around and laugh
and chat about the weather.
Baby cousin Matthew
settles down to take a nap.
He's drowsy, but he's feeling fine,
curled up in my dad's lap.
Mom snaps loads of photos
and everybody smiles.
Warming up to family
sometimes just takes a while.

Soy what?

My aunt is a strict vegetarian.
She refuses to eat any meat.
No burgers, baloney, or bratwurst.
No barbecue ribs for a treat.
She hopes I grow up to be like her.
But I fear that her wish won't come true.
I'm telling you now that I'd rather eat cow
than that goo that my aunt calls tofu.

Ew . . .

Fire**dON't**works

Don'tcha hate dud fireworks?
You light the fuse
and sit and muse:
Will it go bang
or just diffuse?

You reach to check
but, wait, oh heck!
It might still blow
and then—oh no!
Where, oh where
would your finger go?

You wait some more
and ponder how
it didn't go.
But will it now?
It surely might.
It's been so long.
Oh, man. It's a dud.
Crud.

BOOM!

Er, never mind.

Blue Sky

Blue Eyes

Blue Cheese?

Blue Jeans

Blue Cheese

Blue cheese, ew cheese,
smelly, nasty goo cheese.
Yellow cheese? I'll take a bite.
I'll even nibble cheese that's white.
But cheese that's blue? That isn't right.
So, please, don't feed me blue cheese.

The Garden Snake

The garden snake, the garden snake.
The most wonderful snake
that God did make.
He gardens all summer,
and make no mistake,
no one can grow a garden
like a garden snake.

The adder snake adds.
The rattlesnake rattles.
The king snake fights himself
some kingly battles.
Other kinds of snakes are just fine I s'pose,
but they don't plant celery in perfect rows.

The garden snake is perfectly grand.
Who else could plant a garden
without any hands?

Rain, Rain, Rain

Oh, the rain is such a pain
when it's falling from the sky
and we want to be out playin'
and we'd like a little dry.

Oh, the rain is such a pain.
And it wouldn't come, I bet,
if our garden were a-wiltin'
and we'd like a little wet!

Hippo-what-a-mess!

When dealing with more than one wild hippopotamus,
you don't say hippo-ton and, no, not hippo-lot-a-mus.
You don't say hippo-we or even hippo-pot-am-us.
But more than one is hippopotam-i. Why?

When dealing with only one wild hippopotamus,
you don't say hippo-one or even hippo-not-as-much.
Yet to say hippo-pot-am-i would fit without a lot of fuss.
But, no, alas, just one is called a hippopotam-US.

NOSY

I'm a very nosy person,
which is great for smelling roses.
You see, I'm very nosy
cuz I've got a dozen noses.

If you ever come to a dead-end road,
you'll take it, if you're smart.
For just past every end that's dead
is a fresh, alive new start.

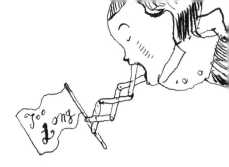

peep
peep

So Long
for Now

We see you've made it to the end.
We say, "So long for now, my friend."
We hope that you've enjoyed your trip
and found these pages fun to flip.
Perhaps someday you'll take a look
if we choose to create another book.
We'd rather not just say "the end."
Instead . . .

bye-
bye

Signing
off!

So Long

ciao

So long for now,
my friend.

[signatures] Karen Wilson & Bare Bell

Game Over!

Humph!

Index of Titles

Index of First Lines